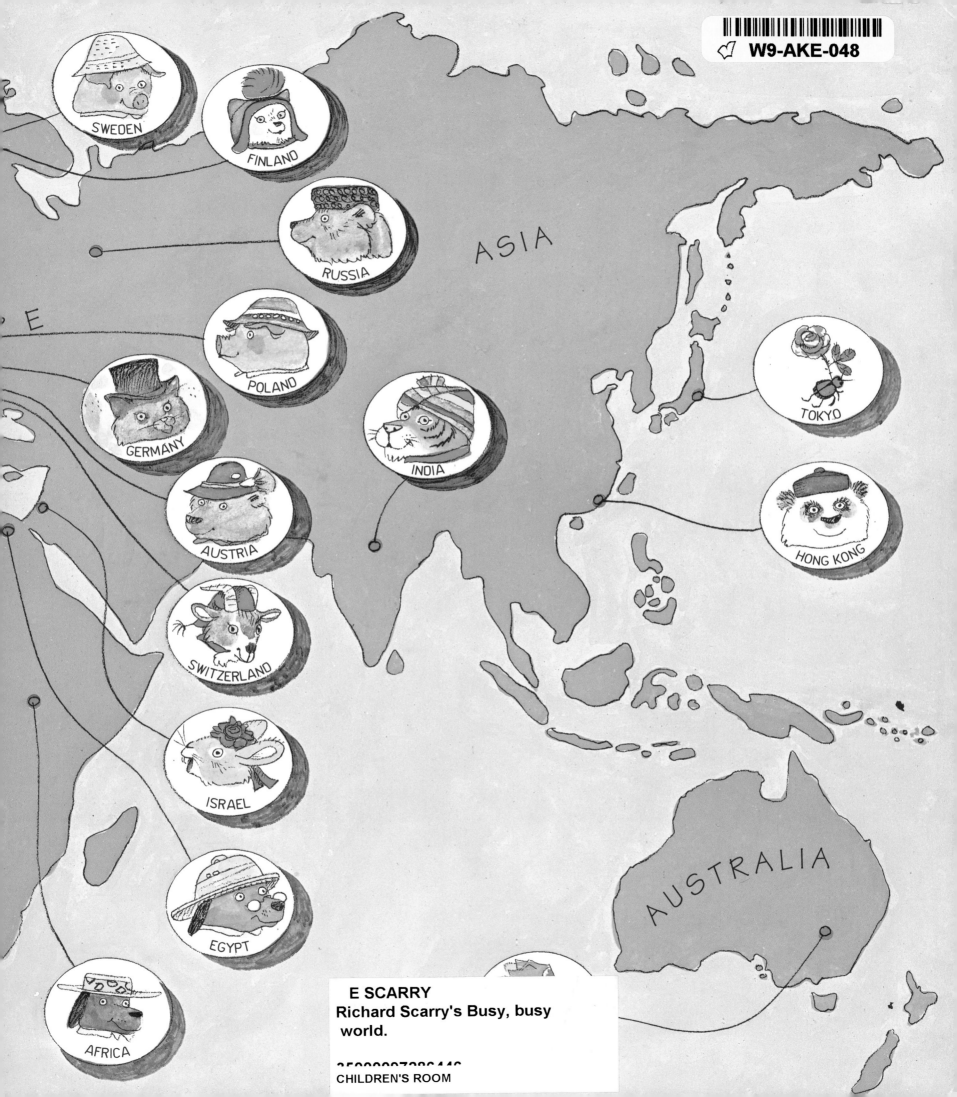

Richard Scarry's

BUSY, BUSY WORLD

A GOLDEN BOOK • NEW YORK

CONTENTS

PIP PIP
GOES TO LONDON

Pip Pip Cat went to London
to seek his fame and fortune
in the service of the Queen.

First, he went to the Tower of London
to see if he could be
a Beefeater, which means
a Guardian of the Queen's jewels.
No! They didn't need any more guards.

When he went to the Queen's palace
the guard wouldn't talk to him.
He was too busy guarding the Queen.

At the Admiralty,
where they guard
the Queen's Navy,
he was afraid of
being stepped upon
and so he quickly left.

Pip Pip was very sad. He wouldn't be able to serve the Queen after all.

"The Queen must be very sad too," he said to himself. "She has lost her ring."

He passed a fountain into which people had thrown pennies for good luck. He saw something which didn't look like a penny! It was golden! It glittered!

It was a ring!
Maybe it was the Queen's ring!!
He showed it to a policeman.

They hurried off to see the Queen. It was the Queen's ring! She was very happy to have it back.

The Queen made Pip Pip "The Queen's Guard of Her Majesty's Fountains."

Every day, he scooped out the "good luck" pennies.

The Queen used the money to buy food for the poor stray cats who had no homes and lived in alleys.

Wasn't she a nice Queen?

COUSCOUS, THE ALGERIAN DETECTIVE

Couscous was the best detective in Algiers. He was very good at disguising himself to look like someone else.

Couscous is in disguise as he walks past the robber's den of Pepe le Gangstair. He is trying to think of a way to get inside the robber's den and capture Pepe and his band of dirty rats.

Can you tell which one is Couscous? No! You can't—because Couscous is so good at disguising himself!

Suddenly Couscous had a good idea. He hurried back to the police station, where his cat and mouse assistants were waiting. He took off his disguise and told them of his plan.

"You have a very clever plan, Couscous!" they all agreed.

That night when it was dark, a small group came to the door of the robber's den and knocked. Knock! Knock! Knock!

"Who is knocking at my door?" growled Pepe le Gangstair. "It is I, the pretty dancing girl Fatima with my troupe of musicians," a soft sweet voice answered. "We have come to entertain you."

"Come in, come in," said Pepe. He opened the door and let them in.

Oh, how beautifully Fatima danced! She was magnificent!

"MORE! MORE!" shouted Pepe.

"I have more for you," said Fatima, "but first I must blindfold you, as I have a big surprise."

So she blindfolded Pepe and the robbers led them out of the door . . .

. . . into the police wagon!

The robbers were prisoners! They had been captured by that clever master of disguise COUSCOUS!!!

My! That Couscous is a clever fellow.

11

ERNST, THE SWISS MOUNTAIN CLIMBER

Ernst Goat could climb up mountains. He could climb down mountains, too.

Heidi Goat had a cow who could climb up mountains. But her cow couldn't climb down.

One day when Ernst was playing his long alphorn Heidi came running and said, "My cow has climbed the mountain again!"

Ernst climbed up the mountain.

"This is the last time I will bring Heidi's cow down from the mountain," he said.

He tied a rope around the cow and started to lower her to the meadow below.

Suddenly he slipped! . . .

. . . and fell!!!!

Ernst caught a branch with his axe just in time.

"I will never again climb that mountain to bring your cow down," he said.

The very next day, Heidi came to Ernst and said, "My cow has climbed the mountain again!"

Ernst grabbed his rope and axe. "This is the last time I will bring your cow down from the mountain," he said.

I wonder if it was?

13

SERGEANT YUKON OF THE CANADIAN "MOUNTIES"

It was a peaceful day in Goldtown away up in the Canadian Northwest. The door to Sergeant Yukon's police station suddenly flew open.

"Klondike Kid and Tundra Pete are back in town!" said Grubstake Moose. That meant trouble, for they were the two meanest men in all Canada.

Sergeant Yukon ran to the door and looked out.

Everyone was running down the street as fast as he could go. Everyone was afraid of those two bullies.

But Sergeant Yukon wasn't afraid. "I shall take care of them," he said to himself as he marched bravely up the street.

Just look at the ugly Klondike Kid. He has taken a lollipop away from a little girl and she is crying.

And just look at that mean Tundra Pete, splashing that nice old lady's dress.
Oh. Doesn't he think he's funny!

"You are both mean bullies," said Sergeant Yukon. "I am taking you to jail." But look out, Sergeant Yukon! I think they mean to hit you!

Sergeant Yukon ducked just in time.

Sergeant Yukon dragged them off to jail. And they stayed there until they learned not to be bullies anymore.

15

A CASTLE IN DENMARK

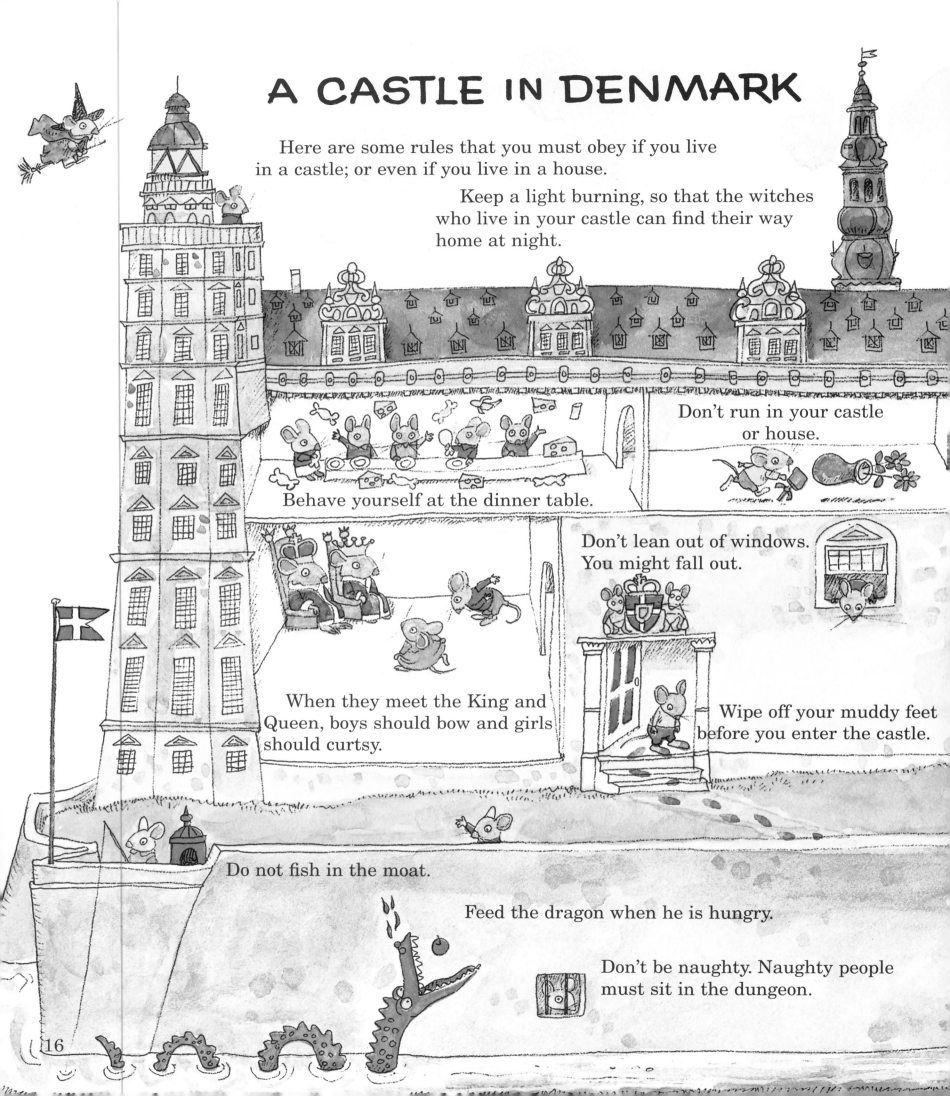

Here are some rules that you must obey if you live in a castle; or even if you live in a house.

Keep a light burning, so that the witches who live in your castle can find their way home at night.

Don't run in your castle or house.

Behave yourself at the dinner table.

Don't lean out of windows. You might fall out.

When they meet the King and Queen, boys should bow and girls should curtsy.

Wipe off your muddy feet before you enter the castle.

Do not fish in the moat.

Feed the dragon when he is hungry.

Don't be naughty. Naughty people must sit in the dungeon.

16

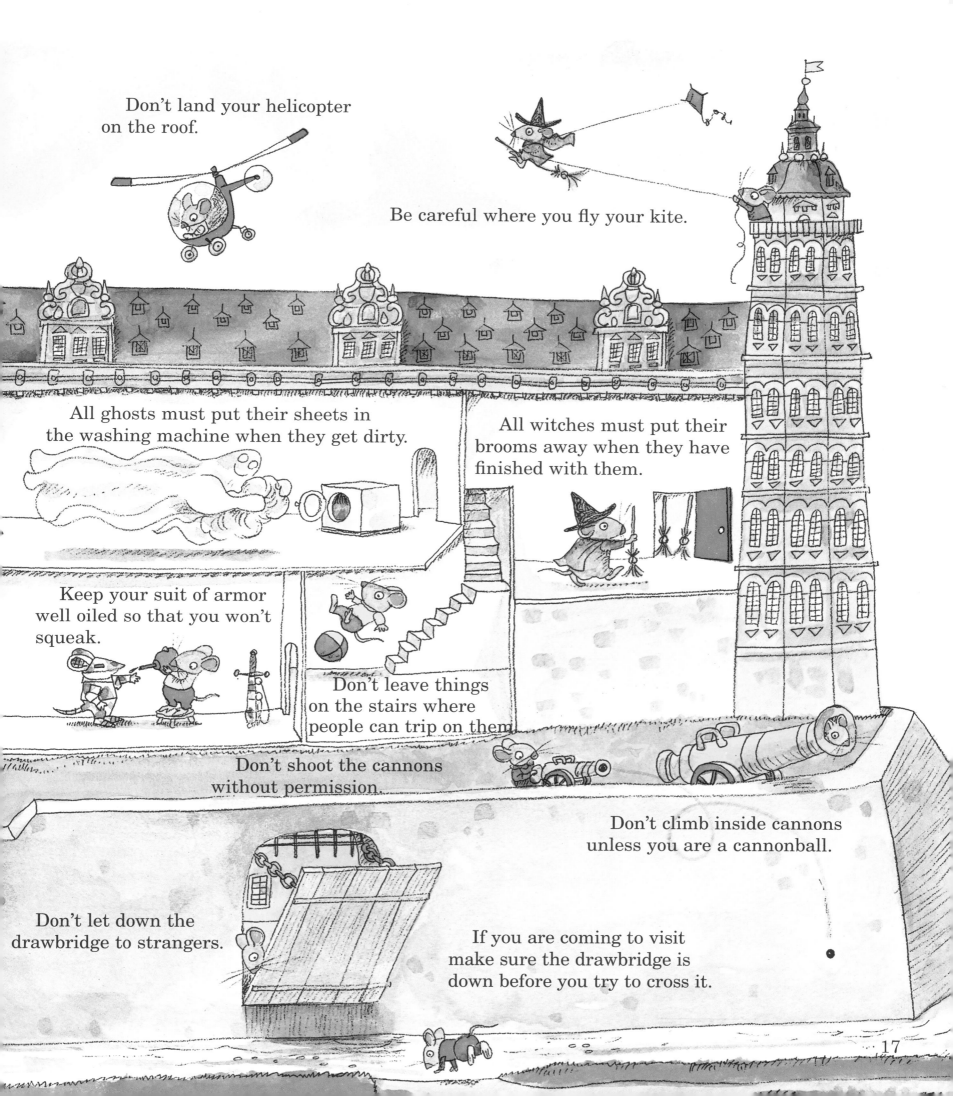

Don't land your helicopter on the roof.

Be careful where you fly your kite.

All ghosts must put their sheets in the washing machine when they get dirty.

All witches must put their brooms away when they have finished with them.

Keep your suit of armor well oiled so that you won't squeak.

Don't leave things on the stairs where people can trip on them.

Don't shoot the cannons without permission.

Don't climb inside cannons unless you are a cannonball.

Don't let down the drawbridge to strangers.

If you are coming to visit make sure the drawbridge is down before you try to cross it.

17

SCHMUDGE, THE GERMAN CHIMNEY SWEEP

Schmudge cleaned the soot from chimneys and quite naturally he got very dirty every day. He looked like a little cloud of black smoke as he walked down the street.

He came to Frau Wascherwommen's house to clean her chimney. She just loved to have things clean. Why, she had just washed her laundry and was putting it out to dry.

"Oh, goody," she said. "Go up to the roof, but don't you dare put any paw prints on my clean walls!"

Schmudge walked up to the roof. The Frau's little boy Hans followed him.

Schmudge walked out onto the roof and looked to see how dirty the chimney was. It was very dirty! Little Hans couldn't see where he was going.

"ACHTUNG!!" shouted a boy who was passing by on his bicycle. "ACHTUNG!! LOOK OUT!!"

Oh, too late! Little Hans
had slipped and fallen!

Brave Schmudge leaped after him
. . . and caught him!!

Down, down they fell . . . into
Frau Wascherwommen's clean white
laundry!

Frau Wascherwommen came running
out of her kitchen.
"You have ruined my laundry,"
she shrieked.

But when she saw that Schmudge
had saved her little Hans she didn't
care.
Schmudge went home . . .

. . . and took a bath!

19

HANS, THE DUTCH PLUMBER

Hans lived in Holland. Somehow or other Hans always managed to come home from work soaking wet. This made his wife very angry.

Sometimes he would get wet because he forgot his umbrella.

Sometimes he would get wet fixing a leaky pipe.

But he really got wet when he didn't look where he was going and fell into a canal.

Now much of the land of Holland is below the level of the sea. The people built dikes to keep the sea water out. If a dike were to get a hole in it, the water would pour through the hole and all the land would be covered with water and fish.

One day Hans saw a big leak in the dike. There was water pouring through it. A tourist was waiting to take a picture of someone putting something in the hole to stop the leak in the dike.

Hans put the tourist in the hole to stop the leak in the dike. Now a tourist is not the best thing for fixing leaks so Hans rode off to get some bags of sand. When he returned he took the tourist out of the hole and filled the hole with bags of sand.

The burgomaster gave Hans a medal. His wife would be very pleased. He had fixed the biggest leak ever and he hadn't got the littlest bit wet.

On his way home it started to rain. He had remembered to bring his umbrella. He would arrive home nice and dry. Today his wife wouldn't be angry with him.

But wait! Hans doesn't see that the bridge is open!

His wife is very angry.

PIERRE,
THE PARIS POLICEMAN

Pierre was directing traffic when
suddenly he heard someone shout,
"Stop that robber! Stop that robber!"
A robber had stolen some jewels from
a store. The robber ran to his car.

22

23

Pierre hopped on his bicycle and chased
after the robber. He blew his whistle
furiously. Brrrrrrreeeeeeeeeet!

Through the crowded streets they raced.

Suddenly the robber's car
crashed into a sidewalk cafe.
The robber ran into the restaurant.
Brrrrrrrrreeeeeeeeet!

Pierre followed him.
Brrrrrrrrreeeeeeeeeet . . .

26

. . . into the kitchen.
"Where is the robber?"
he roared at the chef.
The chef hadn't seen any robber.

Poor Pierre! He had lost
the robber.
"Mmmmmmm, that soup you are
cooking smells good," said Pierre.
"May I taste it?"

He put in his paw.
Look at what he found!
The robber! The robber
had hidden in the soup.

Before Pierre took the robber
away to be punished, they all had
some soup.
"This is the best soup ever!"
said the chef to the robber.
"Perhaps after you have been
punished for stealing, you will
come back and help me make soup
all the time? We will call
it 'Robber Soup.'"
Everyone thought that that
was a good idea.

27

PROFESSOR DIG
AND HIS EGYPTIAN MUMMY

Professor Dig had been out on the desert all day digging.

He dug and dug, until finally, to his great joy, he dug up a beautiful mummy!

He would bring it to the Cairo museum where everyone could come and look at it and say, "OOH! AAH!"

It was *that* beautiful.

The Professor was very hot and thirsty when he arrived in Cairo.

He decided that he would stop at Ali Baba's restaurant to have cold lemonade.

"Will you watch my mummy for a few minutes while I sit and drink a cold glass of lemonade?" the Professor asked Ali Baba.

Now, Ali Baba couldn't see very well. He thought that the professor's MUMMY was the Professor's real live MOTHER!!

"What kind of a son is that who will leave his mother standing after a hot trip while he sits down and has a cold lemonade?" Said Ali to the mummy, "You must be very tired. Permit me to sit you in a chair."

Ali Baba put the mummy in the chair. "Oh you poor woman," said Ali. "You are so stiff from your long journey you can't even bend to sit down. Perhaps if you were to lie down with your feet in the air you would feel better."

"Ah, yes, I can see you are looking better already," he said. "Your dress is a little dusty, though. Let me dust you off. Yes, you are looking much, much better."

"Ah, the music is playing in the Palm Room. Dum de dum de dum. May I have this dance while we are waiting for your son? Dum de dum. Ah, madam, you are a delightful dancer."

Just then the Professor came along. He thanked Ali for taking care of his mummy and carried it away.

"Oh, how that boy treats his poor old mother," said Ali. "IMAGINE!! carrying her on his head! I wouldn't treat my mummy that way! Would YOU?"

29

MARIO, THE VENETIAN GONDOLIER

Mario had a melon boat. Now, a melon boat is very useful, but it is not beautiful, like a gondola. Mario worked hard selling melons, so that one day he would have enough money to buy a beautiful gondola.

"Just look at that pretty gondola all decorated with flowers," he said to himself. "It must be going to a wedding."

Sure enough! The gondola stopped at a palace. Tina, who was a very beautiful princess, came out with her father. The gondola would take her to church to be married.

Oh! What a shame! Tina is too big for the gondola! How will she ever get to the church to be married?

Have no fear. Here comes Mario! He is strong because he is always lifting melons. He lifts Tina and her father into his boat.

Mario rowed them to the church. Everyone thought it was very funny to see all the melons going to a wedding.

Tina was married to Toni. She was so happy she kissed Toni. Tina's father was so happy he kissed Mario. If it hadn't been for Mario there would have been no wedding.

Tina's father gave Mario a shiny new gondola as a present. Mario put his melon boat away in his cellar. He is now a real gondolier. He sings happily as he paddles along the Grand Canal on romantic moonlit nights. But whenever there is a holiday, Mario brings out his melon boat.

For you see . . .

. . . Tina and Toni now have lots of children, and they need a strong and sturdy boat to carry them. Yes! A very strong and sturdy boat!

AH-CHOO OF HONG KONG

Ah-Choo had a nose
that sometimes tickled.

And when it tickled
Ah-Choo sneezed.
AH-CHOOOO!

And when he sneezed
terrible things happened.

Ah-Choo was bringing home
two baskets of eggs. He looked
to see if he had broken any.
No. He hadn't.
His nose tickled again.

Ah-Choo sneezed even louder.
AH-CHOO!

Ah-Choo's eggs didn't break.
But his nose did tickle again.

AH-CHOO!

It is lucky that no one was hurt.
It is lucky the eggs didn't break.

Ah-Choo finally arrived home. Mama and Baby Ah-Choo were waiting. Mama Ah-Choo had her cooking pot on the stove. She was going to cook hard-boiled eggs for supper.

Then what do you think happened?
Baby Ah-Choo sneezed a tiny AH-CHOO!

"I think that for supper we will have dropped-egg soup instead!" said Mama Ah-Choo.

35

DR. KRUNCHCHEW OF RUSSIA

On Monday Dr. Krunchchew fixed Lion's teeth.

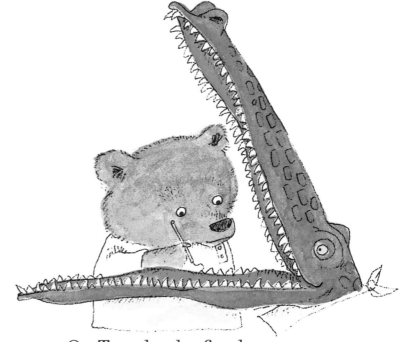

On Tuesday he fixed Alligator's teeth.

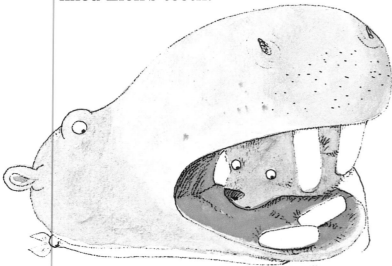

On Wednesday he looked at Hippopotamus' teeth.

On Thursday, Walrus asked Dr. Krunchchew, "Don't you ever get tired of looking at teeth?"

"Certainly not!" said Dr. Krunchchew.

"I LOVE teeth!"

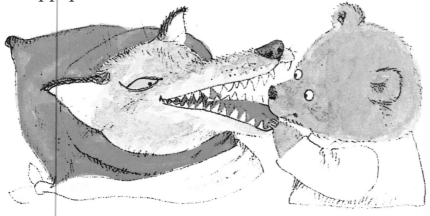

On Friday he cleaned a nice old Grandmother's teeth.

"What have you been eating lately, Grandma?" he asked. Grandma wouldn't say. She just giggled.

"Very fine molars you have, Mr. Mole," laughed Dr. Krunchchew on Saturday.

On Sunday Mrs. Krunchchew said, "You have been looking at teeth all week. You need a rest. Go and look at something different. Why don't you go to the Natural History Museum and look at birds and flowers and other things?"

So Dr. Krunchchew went to the museum, and looked at birds and flowers . . . and . . .

. . . and other things.

OFFICER MONTEY OF MONACO

Police Officer Montey is everyone's friend. He is very smart.
He says:

"Never throw anything at someone.
You might hurt him."

"Cross the street at the cross walk.
"Always look both ways to see that no cars are coming.
Don't run! Always walk!"

"Never, never play where there is deep water. There might not be anyone around to pull you out!"

"Never push or hit anyone.
No one likes a bully."

DANGER

38

"Never lean out of a car window."

"Never chase a ball into the street."

"Play on the sidewalk or in your yard. Never play in the street."

"Never go anywhere with someone you don't know."

"Behave yourself and act like a little lady or gentleman when you are in a car."

"And whatever you do, don't bring home stray alligators! They might bite!"

39

TWO NORWEGIAN FISHERMEN

Uncle Olaf and Uncle Oscar had nine nieces and nephews waiting for them on the dock. They were waiting for Uncle Olaf and Uncle Oscar to catch a big fish for supper.

Uncle Olaf caught a tin can. Uncle Oscar didn't catch anything.

Uncle Olaf caught a rubber boot. Uncle Oscar didn't catch anything.

Uncle Olaf caught an auto tire. Uncle Oscar didn't catch anything. What kind of a fisherman is Uncle Oscar anyway? He can't catch anything.

WOW!! Uncle Oscar caught a fish.

He paddled back to the dock where
the nine nieces and nephews were
waiting . . .

. . . and that night, they had the best fish supper ever!

RAJAH OF INDIA

Rajah was a soldier from India.
One day, a fortune teller said to
Rajah, "Today something will come
from above that will make your wife
very happy."

As he walked through the streets,
Rajah wondered what it might be that
would come from above.

All day long, nothing came from above that would make his wife happy. He was angry with the fortune teller.

Rajah went back to the fortune teller and said, "You told me that something would come from above that would make my wife very happy, and I haven't seen it yet."

"The day is not over yet," said the fortune teller.

Rajah went home to his wife.

"You dear sweet man," she said. "You brought me flowers!"

Just as the fortune teller said, she was very happy.

SOUTH AMERICAN CARNIVAL

Everyone was going to fly to the carnival in the beautiful city of Rio de Janeiro A carnival is such fun!

Everyone was going to sing and to dance and to eat. Everyone, that is, but Noah, the Boa Constrictor. He didn't care much for singing, and he had no feet to dance with. He was just going to eat.

The plane was full and ready to take off. But, just at the last minute, Aunty Ant came running. "There is always room for one more," said the stewardess.

Oh me! Oh my! She was wrong!
That little Aunty Ant was just
one too many! The plane split open!
  "How will we ever get to the
carnival now?" they all asked.
  "I think I know how," said Noah.
"Just everyone stay where he is."

Noah just wrapped himself around
that airplane until the rip was all
closed up.

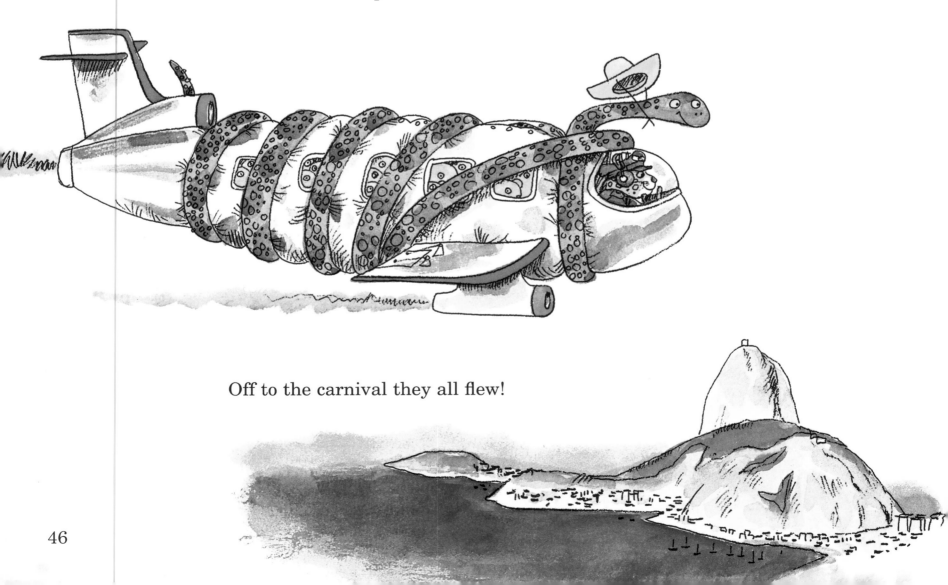

Off to the carnival they all flew!

Everyone had a splendid time.
Everyone sang, and danced, and ate.
Everyone that is, except Noah.
Noah just ate.

SVEN SVENSON'S BUSY DAY

Sven Svenson lived with Mrs. Sven Svenson, on a farm in Sweden. He ate a pickle for breakfast.

He put on his straw hat and he went to the barn to milk his cow. His cow kicked over the milk pail.

He fed his hens and gathered their eggs.

He went to the railroad station to pick up a package which was coming on the train from the city.

It was a present for his wife. He tried it on for fun.

When he got home, he gave the hat to his wife. She gave him a pickle for lunch.

After lunch Sven brought the hay in from the fields. His cow loves to eat hay and straw.

He put the hay into the barn. The wind blew his straw hat up into the barn. He would climb up and get it after he had a drink of water. It was a hot day and he was dry and thirsty.

He went to the well for a drink. He fell in!

Mrs. Svenson came and pulled him out. Her new hat fell in the well.

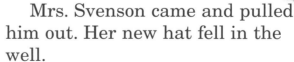

It was the end of a busy day. Sven Svenson and Mrs. Sven Svenson ate seven pickles for supper.

Sven Svenson's cow found
Sven Svenson's hat in
Sven Svenson's barn.
Sven Svenson's cow ate
Sven Svenson's hat for supper.

ALBERT, THE BELGIAN BARGE CAPTAIN

Albert's barge was sailing merrily along the canal. Albert's wife was putting the wash on the line.

Pieter Pig was dreaming of catching a big fish.

"A fish! A fish!
I caught a fish!" said the pig.

"You caught a barge captain!" said Albert. "Now how will I ever get back on my barge?"

48

"There is only one way," said Pieter Pig. "This is the way . . .

. . . to do it!"

Albert's pants ripped.

And Albert landed, upside down, in his pajama pants!

"Why are you wearing your pajamas in the middle of the day?" his wife asked him. "And how *ever* did you tear your nice new pants?"

UKULELE LOUIE,
THE HAWAIIAN FISHERMAN

Every day, Ukulele Louie threw his fishing net into the water.

And every day he pulled his net out of the water. It was always full of fish.

Then gaily singing and playing his ukulele, he took his fish and sold them to his good friend, Joe, who owned a restaurant.

"I wish I could be a cook in a restaurant instead of fishing every day," Louie said to Joe. "I could make all kinds of good things to eat. Yum, yum!"

"Very well," said Joe. "Put on this cook's hat, and go into the kitchen and see what you can cook up. I have to go out but I will be back in a few minutes. Just try to be neat."

Joe left and Louie went into the kitchen.

He put the fish in the refrigerator. He knocked over the milk while he was taking out some eggs.

He poured a jar of vinegar into a bowl. He put two dozen eggs in the bowl, and beat them with a beat egger.

He went to the sink to wash the beat egger. He forgot to turn the faucet off.

He tried to shake some ketchup into the bowl but it wouldn't come out. He shook and shook. The ketchup came out.

He carried the bowl across the kitchen. The door opened.

Joe had returned.

"I am afraid you will never be a good cook," said Joe. "You should have used the applesauce instead of ketchup."

"Yes. I think you are right," said Louie.

And so Ukulele Louie went back to fishing, and singing, and playing his ukulele, and he never wanted to cook anything ever again.

53

54

GOOD LUCK IN ROME

Federico and Maria were visiting Rome for the very first time. They had heard of a fountain that is supposed to bring you good luck if you throw a coin into it.

Federico stopped his car and got out to ask two carabinieri how to get there.

Now for some reason that can't be explained . . .

55

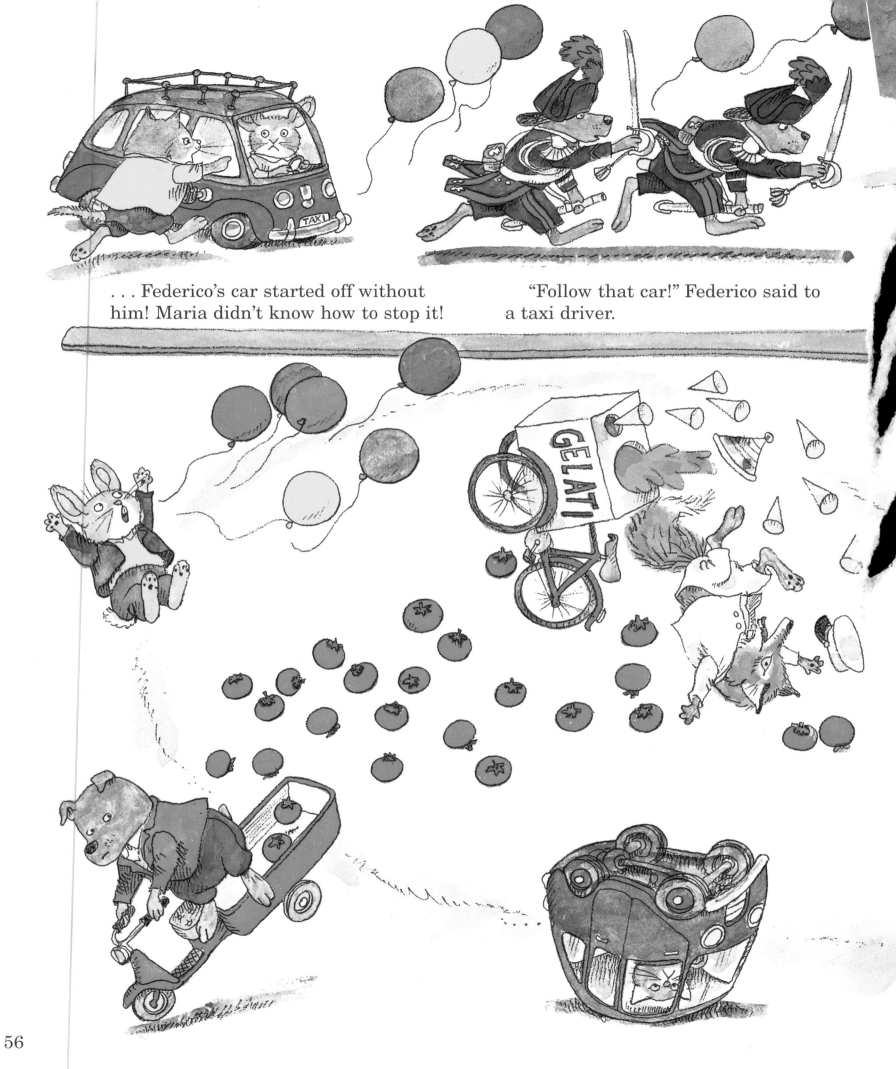

. . . Federico's car started off without him! Maria didn't know how to stop it!

"Follow that car!" Federico said to a taxi driver.

"Help! Help!"
said Maria.

Into St. Peter's Square the little red car raced.
The Swiss Guards were called out to stop it.
But they were too late.

Down the Spanish Steps
they tumbled.

Down narrow streets . . .
. . . into the very fountain
they were looking for.

"You will surely have good luck,"
said the carabinieri. "Most people
have good luck by putting only a
penny in the fountain. But look!
You have put your car in! Yes,
you will surely have good luck!"

MANUEL OF MEXICO

Manuel's wife broke her cooking pot. She needed a new pot to cook her beans in for supper.

"Manuel," she said. "Take this money and go to the market place. Buy a new cooking pot so that you may have hot beans for supper."

Manuel was so excited to be going to the market place. He didn't look where he was going. He kicked a cooking pot by accident and broke it. He paid the man for breaking it.

Pig Lady was cooking beans in her cooking pot. He stepped into the stew by mistake. He said he was sorry.

The smell of Pig Lady's beans made him hungry. He went to Armadillo's restaurant and had a bowl of beans.

When he had finished he accidentally knocked over the bean pot and spilled the beans.

"I think it is time to go home," he said to himself. "I think I am forgetting something but I can't remember what."

He didn't look where he was going and bumped into Dog.

A pot landed on his head. "Ah, yes, I remember now. I was to buy a cooking pot," Manuel said to himself.
But alas! The pot was stuck on his head.

He went home to his wife. "I remembered to bring home a cooking pot," he said.

His wife had to break the pot to get it off his head.
Manuel had cold beans for supper.

GLIP AND GLOP, THE GREEK PAINTERS

Mrs. Metropolus asked Glip and Glop to come and paint her house.

She didn't care what colors they painted it on the inside. But she did insist that the outside of the house be painted blue and white.

She asked Glip and Glop to mind her little boy, Percy, while she went shopping.

"Remember! Paint the outside blue and white," she said as she left.

Glip painted the living room. It was beautiful.

Glop painted a funny wolf on Percy's bedroom wall.

They both painted a happy sun on the dining-room ceiling.

And when they had finished painting the inside of the house they went outside to paint the outside of the house.

"Don't forget . . . blue and white," Glip said to Glop.

Glip painted two sides of the house blue and white.

And Glop painted two sides of the house blue and white.

Oh look what they have done! They have painted the house blue and white all right. But half the house has blue sides with white windows, and the other half has white sides with blue windows.

Mrs. Metropolus would be furious.

But when Mrs. Metropolus came home, she was very pleased. "Why, it is just like having two houses," she said.

That night she gave Percy a bath.

CUCUMBER, THE AFRICAN PHOTOGRAPHER

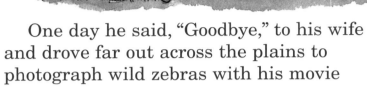

Cucumber took pictures of wild giraffes, and wild zebras, and other wild animals. But he never took pictures of wild lions. Why? Because he was afraid of them!

One day he said, "Goodbye," to his wife and drove far out across the plains to photograph wild zebras with his movie camera.

When nighttime came he set up his tent. After he had eaten his supper and played a few songs on his banjo, he went to sleep.

Cucumber had not been asleep long when some wild animals came into his tent. WILD LIONS!!!

"Look at that cute doll," said the little girl lion.

"I wonder what this machine is for?" said Father Lion.

He pressed a button and the camera started to work.

WHRRRRRRrrrrrrrrr!

Then he picked up Cucumber's banjo
and started to sing.
The little girl lion picked up
Cucumber, and started to dance.
Cucumber was sound asleep.
The twin baby lions started to cry.

"Put the doll back in bed,"
roared Mother Lion. "It is time
we were leaving."

The little girl lion put Cucumber
back in his bed. Even with all
that noise and everything, Cucumber
didn't wake up.

"WHRRRrrr! Clop!"
The camera stopped working.

In the morning Cucumber drove home.
What a surprise, when he showed his
wife the moving pictures!
"Why, you were only fooling!" said
Mrs. Cucumber. "You're not afraid of
wild lions after all."
And Cucumber never was after that.

67

TAKING THE TOKYO TRAIN

Here is Hunki Dori. He is coming home from nursery school. He is hurrying to get on the train.

Here is Suki Yahki, the Japanese Beetle. He is taking a rose home to his pretty wife.

There are others running to get on the train. Hurry! Hurry! Hurry! Do not miss the train.

Don't push! Don't push!
There is room for everyone!

Who will be first on the train?
It will be Sue Zookie, I think.
She is carrying a big, fat, round
sausage for supper.

Hunki Dori is the last one on the train.
The railway guard SQUEEZES him in.

The train leaves the station. Squinch,
squunch, squooch, squeeze, all the way
home.

Everyone gets off the train at the last station.
Sue Zookie is carrying her big, fat, round sausage.
Oh no! Look at what has happened to her fat sausage!
It has been squinched, squunched, squooched, squeezed.
SQUASHED!
My, what a funny sausage!

69

ANGUS, THE SCOTTISH BAGPIPER

When Officer Angus said "Stop!" people heard him and they stopped!

He told the cars to *STOP* so that the Macintosh family could cross the street. The cars stopped.

He told two silly boys to *stop fighting*. The silly boys stopped.

He told Sandy to please *STOP DANCING* on the grass. Sandy stopped.

He had spent a busy day telling people to stop doing something. Now he was going to go home and have fun playing his bagpipes.

Angus marched about his house playing his bagpipes.

"SCREECH SCREECH OOOHAAAH OOOHAAAAH!"

Oh such a horrible ferocious noise he made!

"NYANNGGGG NYANNGGGG NYANNGGGGGGGG!"

The sound of his bagpipes could be heard all over town.

"Angus, please STOP!" all the people cried. But Angus was playing so loudly he couldn't hear. And the longer he played the louder he played, and the bigger his bagpipe swelled up.

"ANGUS, PLEASE STOP!!!" the people cried even louder. But Angus couldn't hear them.

Louder and louder he played, and bigger and BIGGER his bagpipe grew.

"ANGUS, PLEASE STOP!!!!" the people roared.

Fortunately for the townsfolk, the bagpipe burst, and Angus STOPPED.

71

THE SMART POLISH FARMERS

Farmer Polka kept brown chickens.
He thought they laid better eggs
than spotted chickens.

Farmer Dotta lived next door.
He kept spotted chickens because
he thought they laid better eggs
than brown chickens.

Polka and Dotta spent all their time
arguing when it would have been better
for them if they spent their time
working or playing games together.

One day they were arguing as usual.
"My hens lay better eggs than yours,"
said Polka Pig.
They both put down their pails . . .
. . . and they started to fight!

Oh, silly Polka and
silly Dotta.

72

They fit and they fought.

And when those silly farmers could fight no more they stopped.

They went to pick up their pails of eggs but they couldn't tell which belonged to whom, for the eggs in both pails were exactly alike.

"How silly we have been," they both said, and then they had a good idea. "Let us work and play together and always be friends."

Well, you should see those smart farmers today. They took down the fence between their barnyards. They now have brown chickens, red chickens, black chickens, white chickens, spotted chickens, all kinds of chickens. They even have an ostrich! And they all lay exactly the same eggs. Well—*almost all* of them do.

HAPPY LAPPY FROM FINLAND

Happy Lappy lives in the far north of Finland.

Happy Lappy's father takes care of Santa Claus' reindeer. Just before Christmas every year, he lassoes the reindeer and takes them to Santa.

The reindeer are very strong, and Lappy is too small to lasso them.

"When you are big and strong," his father told him, "you will lasso the reindeer for Santa." To be ready when that day comes, Lappy practices with his rope.

Lappy's sister holds two branches to her head. She pretends she is a reindeer. Lappy chases her. Just as she disappears over the hill, Lappy throws his lasso. He has lassoed her.

74

But no! He has lassoed one of Santa's reindeer and that reindeer didn't want to be lassoed.

Away he ran, with Lappy holding on tight.

Around and around in circles he ran . . . but Lappy didn't let go.

After a while that reindeer was so tired he could run no more.

Lappy's father was so pleased.

"You are now big and strong enough to lasso Santa's reindeer," he said.

"From now on you will take care of them. Come along now. We must take the reindeer to Santa. Perhaps he will have a toy for each of you."

Sure enough, Santa did. Lappy and his sister were very happy.

PATRICK PIG LEARNS TO TALK

It was well known that every Irishman can talk . . . and talk . . . and talk.

But not Patrick Pig. The only thing Patrick could say was, "Oink, oink."

"It is a disgrace that Patrick can't talk," said his father. "We must take him to the Blarney Castle and have him kiss the Blarney stone."

As everyone knows, if you kiss the magic Blarney stone you will be able to talk about anything for hours and hours.

Off to Blarney Castle they went in their little jaunting cart. "Oink, oink," said Patrick.

They climbed to the top of the castle, where the Blarney stone was. Patrick's father held him while he kissed the stone.

"Now let us see if our fine broth of a lad can talk," said Patrick's father.

"UP THE IRISH!!!" shouted Patrick. "Mother Machree, Erin Go Bragh, Macnamarra's band, Lucille Ogle, Kathleen Norah Daly, Sean O'Casey, and Albert Leventhal!"

His mother and father were very pleased.

"Patrick is now a real, talking Irishman," his father said. "Come, it is time to go home."

All the way home Patrick talked.

"The wearin' o' the Green, sure an' begorra, Toora, loora, la," Patrick said.

Then he sang, "Did Your Mother Come from Ireland?" "It's a Long Way to Tipperary," and "When Irish Eyes Are Smiling."

"Will the lad ever stop talking?" Patrick's father wondered.

Patrick started to name all the Kings of Ireland: "King O'Murphy, King O'Toole, King O'Sullivan, King O'Risom. . . ."

Patrick's father said to Patrick's mother,

"Do you know of anything we can do to make him stop talking?"

Patrick's mother thought she knew of a way to make Patrick stop, but she couldn't tell Patrick's father.

For you see, the only word she knew how to say was, "Oink."

And so, Patrick's father never did find out how to make Patrick stop talking!

77

SNEEF, THE BEST DETECTIVE IN EUROPE

Sneef was the best detective in all Europe. He was always ready to help Police Chiefs at any time and in any place.

One rainy day in Paris, Sneef received a phone call from the Chief of Police of Nice. He wanted Sneef to come right away.

Oh! How sad. Tomorrow would be Sneef's birthday and he had hoped to spend it at home eating ice cream and cake.

He ran all the way to the train.

"I wonder who all those bad-looking men are," said Sneef to himself as the train conductor showed him to his bedroom.

"They seem to be watching me!" Sneef was a little frightened.

At every station they stopped at that night, Sneef could see more evil-looking men getting on the train. And they all carried violin cases! What mischief were they up to?

Sneef was very frightened! He shivered and hid under the bed.

The train arrived in Nice in the morning. Sneef crawled out from under the bed and saw those mysterious men looking at him.

Before he got off the train he put on sunglasses to protect his eyes from the bright sunlight.

When he stepped off the train what do you suppose he saw? Why, he saw all the Police Chiefs of Europe!

They had thrown away their disguises and were playing on their violins.

They were playing, "Happy Birthday to You, Dear Sneefy!"

It was a surprise birthday party!

They all went to the beach and ate ice cream and cake until they could eat no more.

It was Sneef's best birthday party ever!

SHALOM OF ISRAEL

Shalom had a wife. She was always shouting at him, "Don't forget to do this, or that!" Poor Shalom.

Now it seems that Shalom was going to build a new house. While he was building it, Mrs. Shalom was going to visit her mother in the city.

As she was leaving, she shouted at Shalom, "Don't forget to put in doors and windows, and everything else that belongs in a house."

"Peace at last!" said Shalom to himself.

Shalom started to build their new house. First, he built the walls with cement blocks. He didn't forget to leave openings for the windows.

Then he put plaster over the blocks.

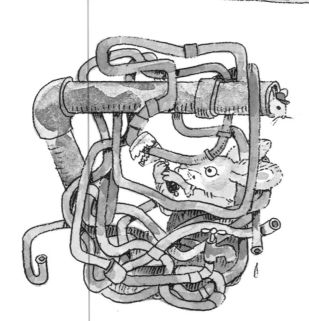

He didn't forget to put in water pipes.

He didn't forget to put in windows.

He put a stove in the kitchen,
. . . a sink in the bathroom
. . . and a telephone
in the living room.

He didn't forget
to build a chimney.

The last thing he did was to put
on a pretty orange roof.
OH! NO! He has forgotten to put
in a door!

What will his wife say when she
comes back?
LOOK! There she comes now!
My! she is a fast driver.

Oh dear SHE FORGOT to stop!
She made a big hole in each end
of the house.

Shalom put a door in one of
the holes she had made. He put a
back door in the other hole.
And never, ever again, did she shout
at him if he forgot something.
Lucky Shalom!

SMOKEY, THE NEW YORK FIREMAN

Smokey was taking a nap in his firehouse.

The fire alarm rang!
BRRRRRRRRRRRRINNNNNNGGGGGG!!

He slid down a pole into his fire engine below.

Look! There is smoke coming from Kathleen Kitty's window!

Smokey put on his hat, his boots, and his raincoat.

Clang! Clang! Get out of the way!
Officer Murphy stopped the cars.

A pie truck didn't get out of the
way in time.
The sky was full of blueberry
pies . . . and the pieman!

Kathleen Kitty was screaming to be saved.

Smokey climbed up the ladder and saved her.

He turned his hose on the fire.
SWOOOOOOOOOOSH!
and the fire was out.

He turned his hose on his fire engine. SWOOOOOOOOSH! and his fire engine was red again.

He turned his hose on the pieman. SWOOOOOOOOOOSH! and the pieman was clean again.

Then they all went inside to see what the fire was all about. It was a blueberry pie that had burned in the oven.

So Kathleen Kitty made another . . .

. . . and they all sat down and ate it.

SCHTOOMPAH, THE FUNNY AUSTRIAN

Schtoompah was a funny fellow. He was not very tidy. Instead of putting things away neatly, he would just throw things in a closet.

He threw his tuba in the closet.

He threw mittens and jackets and rakes into that closet.

He even threw the kitchen stove in by mistake.

And then when he went to look for something he could never find it.

Schtoompah was going to play his tuba for the Saturday night band concert. He spent two whole days looking for his tuba before he finally found it.

Now, he was ready to go to the band concert.

Schtoompah put his tuba on his head, and rode his bicycle backward.

"Oh that Schtoompah, he is a funny fellow," the townspeople all said. "I wonder what funny thing he will do at the band concert?"

The band concert was about to begin. "Uh-eins, uh-zei, uh-drei," said the band leader.

Schtoompah blew, but no music came out.
He blew even harder, but still no music came out.
Schtoompah took a deep breath; and blew with all his might. . . .

87

BLAZZZZZZZZZZZ!
"Oh, that Schtoompah!
He is a funny fellow,"
the townspeople all laughed.

NURSE MATILDA
OF AUSTRALIA

Nurse Matilda was very busy in the hospital. She gave Anteater his medicine for his sore throat.

She put an icebag on Cassowary's head and took his temperature.

She bandaged Bandicoot's ear and gave him a book to read.

She gave Goat a glass of orange juice, and a straw to drink it with.

She put naughty Bunny Rabbit back into bed for the nineteenth time. Isn't he awful! He got out again as soon as she left.

I wonder where Nurse Matilda was going to now?

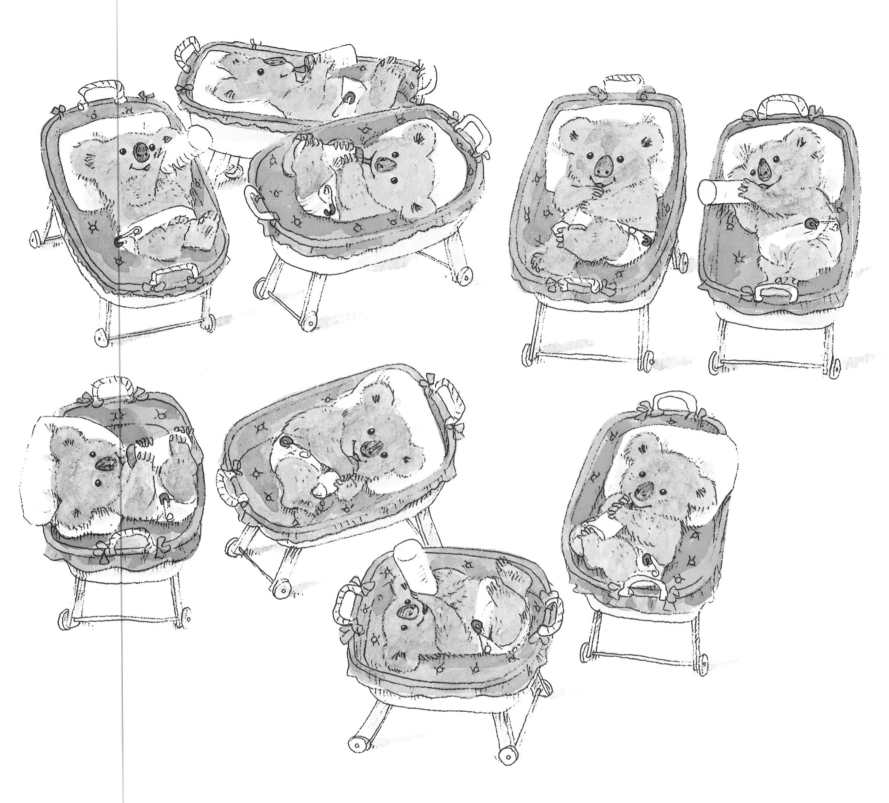

Why, she was going to the nursery
to give the Koala babies their bottles.
Now all the Koala babies are happy with
their bottles. But Nurse Matilda has
one bottle left. Whom can that be for,
I wonder?

Why, of course! It is for her own little baby, Billybong.
Drink it all up, Billybong!

LOOK! Who is that riding home on his bicycle?
WHY! It is Schtoompah!
He has drawn a funny face on his tuba.
My, he is a funny fellow!

THE END

I hope he remembers to put his tuba away
neatly, in his closet, don't you?
 Do you ever forget to put your tuba away
in your closet, before you go to bed?
  Do you?